Ann Jungman studied Law at Exeter University. She later trained as a teacher and has taught at all levels from primary to adult. Author of over fifty children's titles including the bestselling *Vlad the Drac* books (Collins), Ann's commitment to feminism is now a major influence in her writing.

Russell Ayto was born in Chichester, Sussex. He took a degree in Graphic Design at Exeter College of Art, specialising in Illustration. His previous books include *Letter to a Friend* (Puffin), *Harry and the Lady Next Door* (BBC Educational) and *This Little Baby* (Walker). Russell is married and lives in Banbury, Oxfordshire.

For Cressida and Hugh   A.J.
For Lisa and Natalie Mort   R.A.

First published in Great Britain in 1992 by
Frances Lincoln Limited, 4 Torriano Mews
Torriano Avenue, London NW5 2RZ

First paperback edition 1995

British Library Cataloguing in Publication Data
available on request

ISBN 0-7112-0726-7 hardback
ISBN 0-7112-1051-9 paperback

Set in Baskerville
Printed in Hong Kong

3 5 7 9 8 6 4 2

Cinderella
AND THE
Hot Air Balloon

by Ann Jungman
Illustrations by Russell Ayto

FRANCES LINCOLN

Long ago and far away there lived a rich merchant with three daughters.

The two eldest, Ermentrude and Esmerelda, liked to comb their hair, try on clothes, polish their nails, and gossip.

Ella, the youngest, was different. She liked to climb trees, ride horses bareback, skate on thin ice, and run barefoot.

What Ella liked most of all was to talk to Cook and
the other servants round the kitchen fire. Often they
cooked potatoes in the cinders and ate them with
melted butter dripping down their fingers.

"Fancy talking to the servants when you could be
up here with us," sneered Esmerelda.

"You spend so much time among the cinders, we
ought to call you Cinderella," jeered Ermentrude.

Ella laughed. "I wouldn't mind. I'd like it better
than boring old Ella." So from that day on, Ella
was known as Cinderella.

One day a messenger came with invitations to a ball at the palace.

"How wonderful!" cried Esmerelda. "I shall go in green silk and dripping with diamonds."

"I shall wear my purple satin," declared Ermentrude, "and dear Mother's emeralds."

"Boring!" muttered Cinderella. "And I *shan't* go."

On the night of the ball, Esmerelda and Ermentrude were dressed and ready.

"I'd better see where Ella is," sighed their father.

He found her huddled in bed. "I'm feeling ill, father," she cried. "You'll have to go without me. Have a wonderful time."

As the coach drove away, Cinderella leapt out of bed and raced down to the kitchen.

"I didn't want to go to the boring old ball," she explained. "I'd much rather eat potatoes here with you."

At that moment, Cinderella's Fairy Godmother appeared.

"Fear not, Cinderella!" she cried. "You *shall* go to the ball!"

"Oh no, Fairy Godmother," Cinderella begged. "I really don't want to go to the ball."

"You mean you don't want a beautiful ball dress and glass slippers?"

"No," insisted Cinderella. "I've got masses of dresses, but the maids and Cook haven't. Please make ball gowns for them instead."

So the Fairy Godmother did just that.

What's more, at Cinderella's suggestion she turned a pumpkin into a coach and mice into footmen so that the servants could have a real night out.

Soon the maids and Cook were bundled into the coach, and off they went all around the town.

They had so much fun that the next time the coach passed the house, the Fairy Godmother clambered in beside them.

Cinderella stayed in the kitchen to bake potatoes and rustle up some pumpkin soup.

When the travellers got back, they tucked in.

"What now?" asked Cook.

"Let's have our own dance," suggested Cinderella. "Godmother, could you turn some frogs into musicians so we can have our own band?"

"All right," said the Fairy Godmother. "And I'll turn some frogs into young men, so you all have partners to dance with."

The frog band had two trumpets, a double bass,
a set of drums, and the grandest piano you ever saw.

Soon everyone was having the time of their lives.

The neighbours heard the music and came to join
in. Before long there were so many people that the
dance spilled out into the garden and the noise
could be heard at the palace.

The King's guests began to leave the ball to go to
Cinderella's party. After a while, even the King and
Queen came to join in the fun.

Cinderella climbed a tree and watched the party
with great satisfaction.

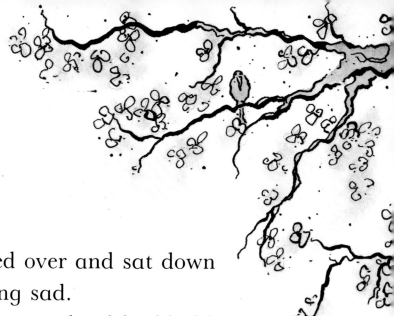

A young man wandered over and sat down beneath the tree, looking sad.

Cinderella swung down to land beside him.

"Hello, I'm Cinderella. This is my party, well, sort of."

"I'm Prince Charming," the young man said with a sigh. "Isn't that the worst name you ever heard?"

"Choose another one then," said Cinderella. "I think people should do what they like."

"I've always dreamed of being called Bill," he told her.

"That's a good name," agreed Cinderella. "Come on, Bill. Let's go and join in the dancing."

"I'll dance if you want to," Bill said, "but to be honest, I don't really like dancing. What I really like is climbing trees, riding bareback, skating on thin ice and running barefoot."

"So do I!" cried Cinderella. "Let's run away together and do the things we like all day long."

"My father wouldn't let me. When he catches up with me I'll be in terrible trouble. Oh no!"

As he spoke Bill caught sight of the King. At the same instant, Cinderella spotted her father and sisters.

"Don't despair, Bill!" Cinderella cried. "Go and find a big pumpkin while I fetch my Fairy Godmother."

She dragged her Fairy Godmother away from the dancing. "Now, Fairy Godmother, I *really* need your help. Please, please turn the pumpkin into a hot air balloon as fast as you can."

The Fairy Godmother waved her wand. There in the middle of the lawn stood a wonderful, multicoloured hot air balloon.

"Get in quick, Bill," yelled Cinderella as the balloon rose into the air.

"Come back this instant," shouted Cinderella's father and sisters.

"Charming, come down this minute," bellowed the King, "or I'll never forgive you."

"Goodbye Cinderella," called the crowd.

Bill and Cinderella waved. "We'll write to you," they shouted. "Byeee!"

And the balloon floated out of sight.

MORE PICTURE BOOKS IN PAPERBACK FROM FRANCES LINCOLN

TATTERCOATS

Margaret Greaves

Illustrated by Margaret Chamberlain

Poor ragged Tattercoats lives in the kitchen of her grandfather's castle. Her only friend is the boy who looks after the geese. But no-one will let *her* go to the ball, when the Prince is looking for a bride... This delightful retelling of a Cinderella-like tale will enchant young readers everywhere.

Suitable for National Curriculum English - Reading, Key Stages 1 and 2
Scottish Guidelines, English Language - Reading, Levels A and B

ISBN 0-7112-0649-X £4.99

CHINYE

Obi Onyefulu

Illustrated by Evie Safarewicz

Poor Chinye! Back and forth through the forest she goes, fetching and carrying for her cruel stepmother. But strange powers are watching over her, and soon her life will be magically transformed... An enchanting retelling of a traditional West African folk tale of goodness, greed and a treasure-house of gold.

Suitable for National Curriculum English - Reading, Key Stages 1 and 2
Scottish Guidelines, English Language - Reading, Level B

ISBN 0-7112-1052-7 £4.99

CAMILLE AND THE SUNFLOWERS

Laurence Anholt

"One day a strange man arrived in Camille's town. He had a straw hat and a yellow beard..." The strange man is the artist Vincent van Gogh, seen through the eyes of a young boy entranced by Vincent's painting. An enchanting introduction to the great painter, with reproductions of Van Gogh's work.

Suitable for National Curriculum English - Reading, Key Stages 1 and 2
Art - Knowledge and Understanding, Key Stage 2
Scottish Guidelines, English Language - Reading, Levels A and B

ISBN 0-7112-1050-0 £4.99

Frances Lincoln titles are available at all good bookshops.

Prices are correct at time of printing, but may be subject to change.